Growing Vegetable Soup

Written and illustrated by
Lois Ehlert

HOUGHTON MIFFLIN HARCOURT · BOSTON NEW YORK

Dedicated to my fellow gardeners:
Gladys, Harry, John, and Jan

www.hmhbooks.com

The Library of Congress has cataloged the hardcover edition of this book as follows:
Ehlert, Lois.
Growing vegetable soup.
Summary: A father and child grow vegetables and then make them into soup.
[1. Vegetable gardening—Fiction. 2. Soups—Fiction.]
I. Title.
PZ7.E44Gr 1987 [E] 86-22812
ISBN: 978-0-15-232575-6 hardcover
ISBN: 978-0-15-232580-0 paperback
ISBN: 978-0-15-232581-7 big book
ISBN: 978-0-15-205055-9 board book
ISBN: 978-0-15-206176-0 lap board book
ISBN: 978-0-544-05275-8 paper-over-board
Manufactured in China
LEO 10 9 8 7 6 5 4 3 2 1
4500390663

Dad says we are
going to grow
vegetable soup.

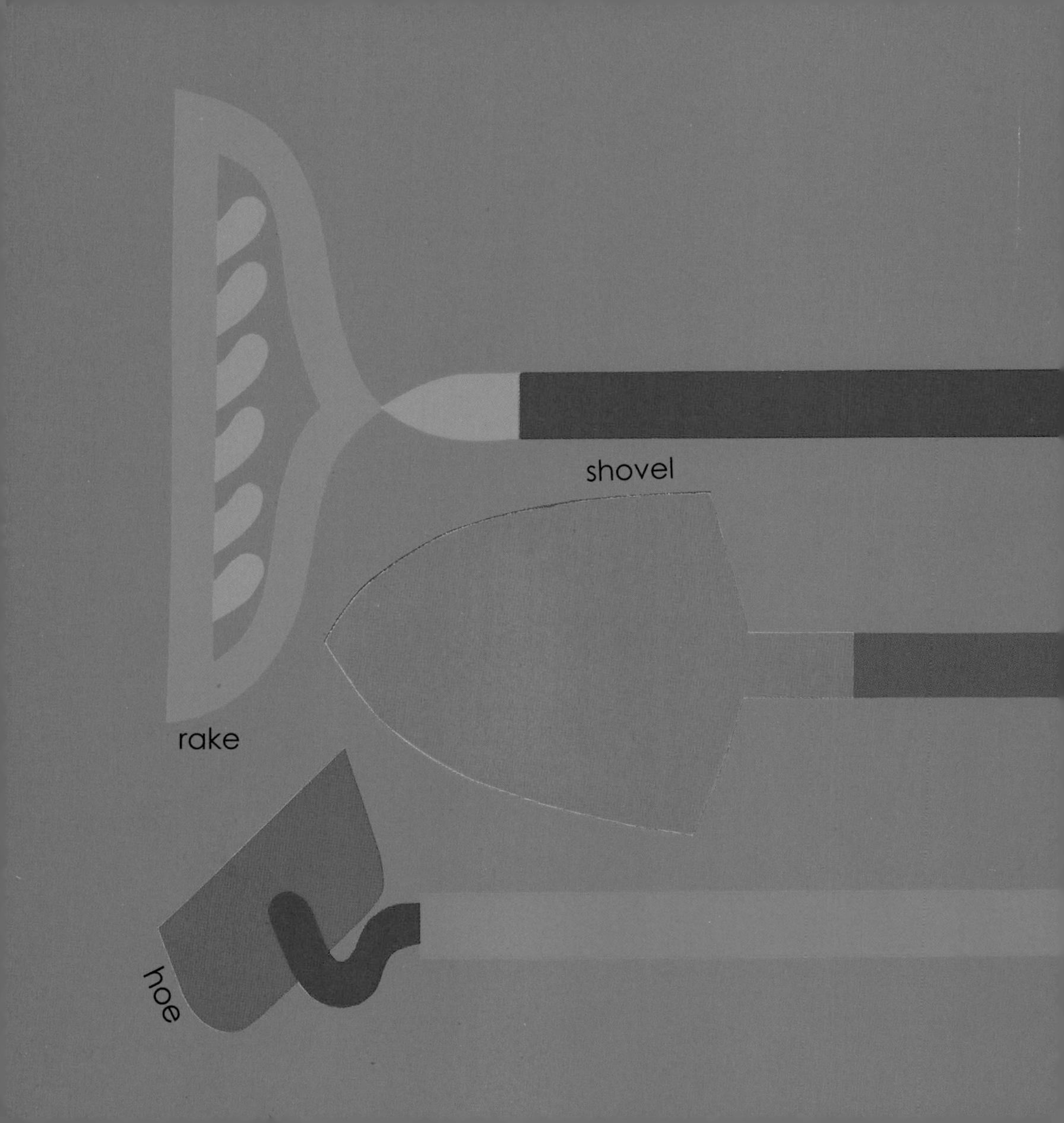
shovel
rake
hoe

We're ready to work,

and our tools are

ready, too.

We are planting

the seeds,

garden glove
een bean seed
pea seed
corn seed
zucchini squash seed
carrot seeds

and all the sprouts,

trowel
PEPPER
CABBAGE
set onions
peat moss pot

watering
TOMATO
POTATO
GREEN BEAN
CARROT
CABBAGE

and giving them water,

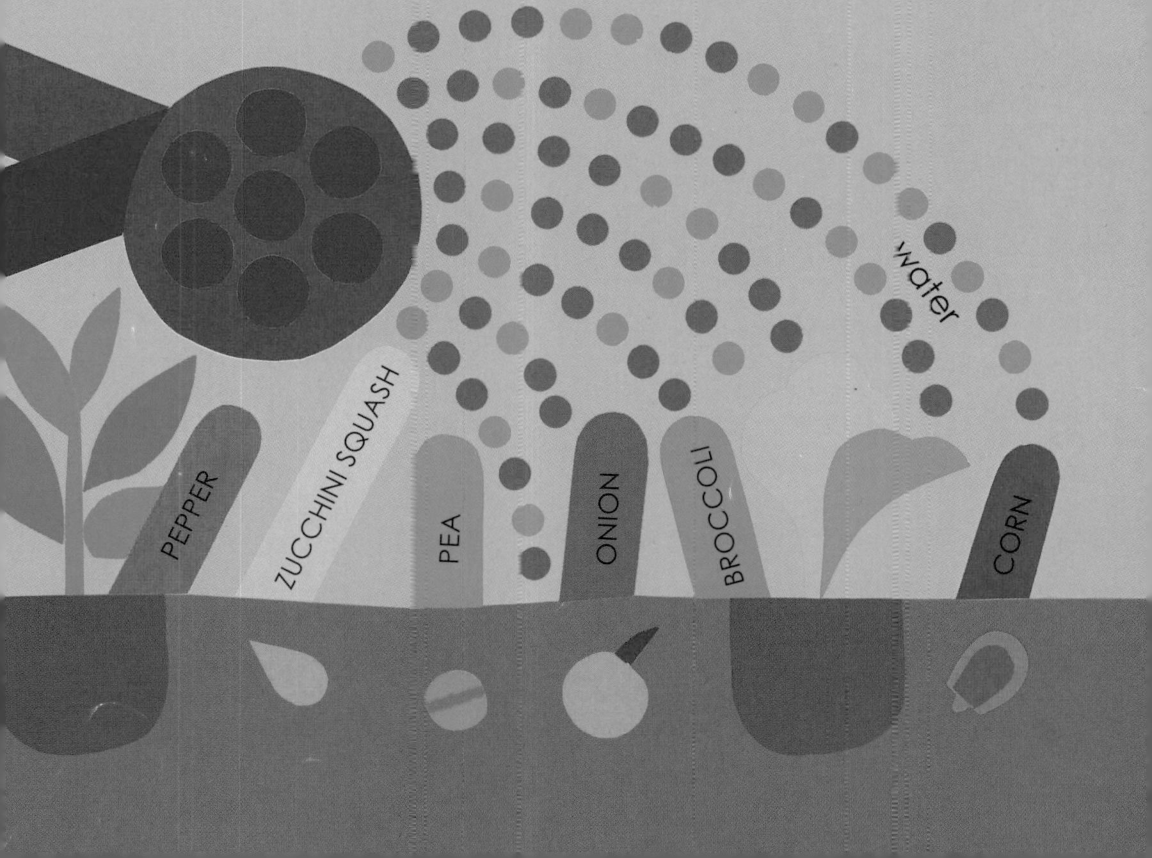

and waiting for warm sun to make them grow,

sun
PEPPER
TOMATO
CABBAGE
GREEN BEAN
BROCCOLI

and grow,

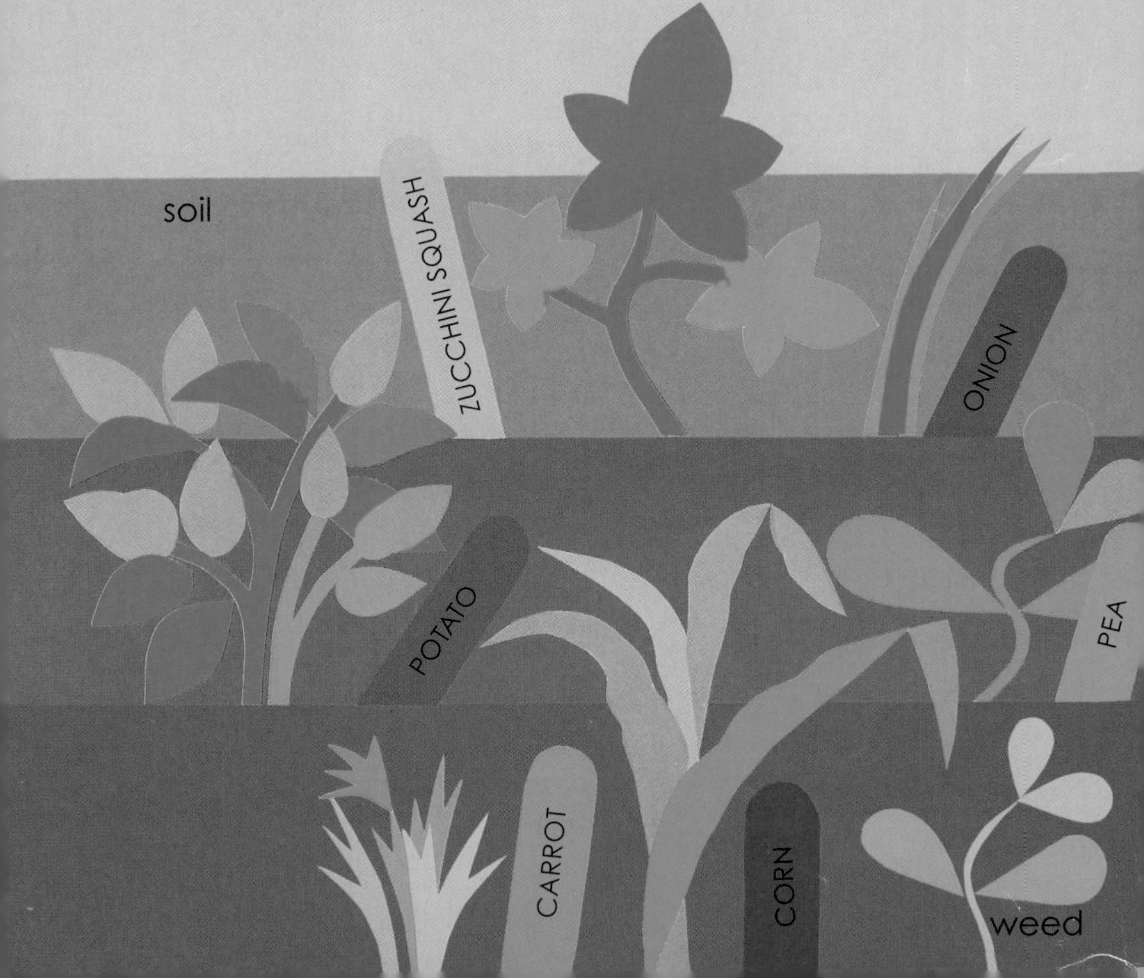

sun
PEPPER
TOMATO
CABBAGE
GREEN BEAN
BROCCOLI

and grow into plants.

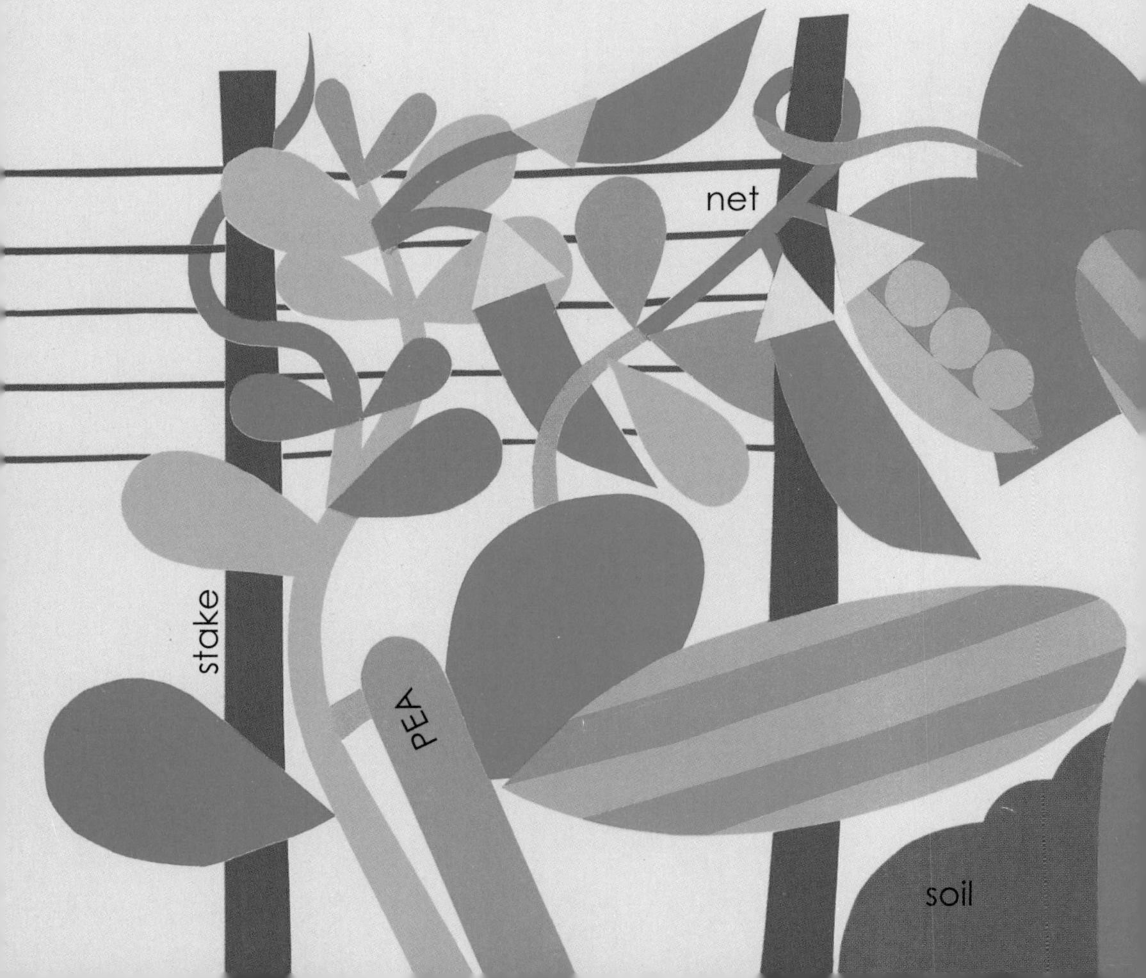

squash
bud
squash
blossom
ZUCCHINI SQUASH

We watch

over them and weed,

until the vegetables are ready for us to pick

pper
corn
hand basket

spadi
fork

or dig up

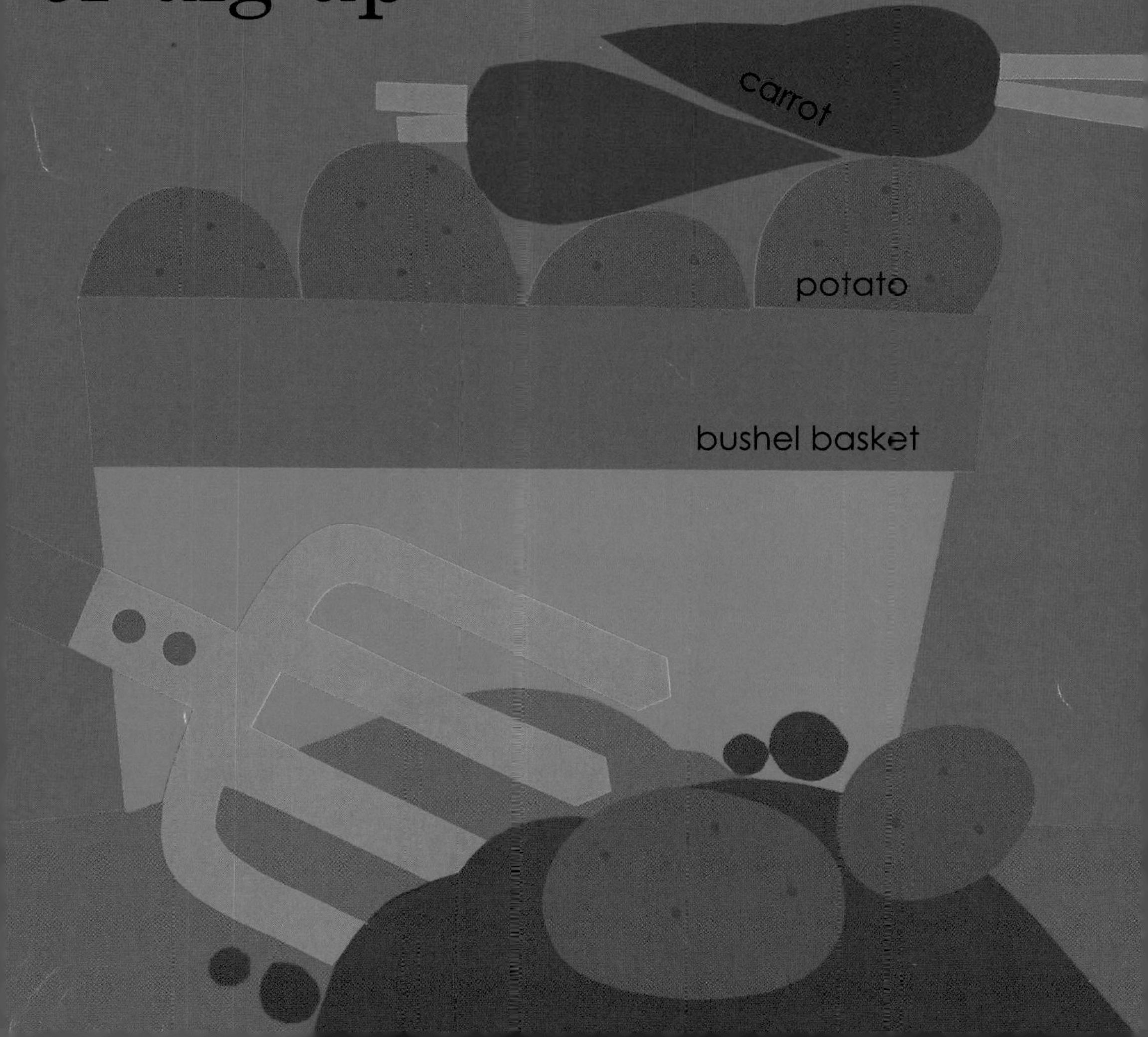

and carry home.
Then we wash them

onion
pail

and cut them and put them in a pot of water,

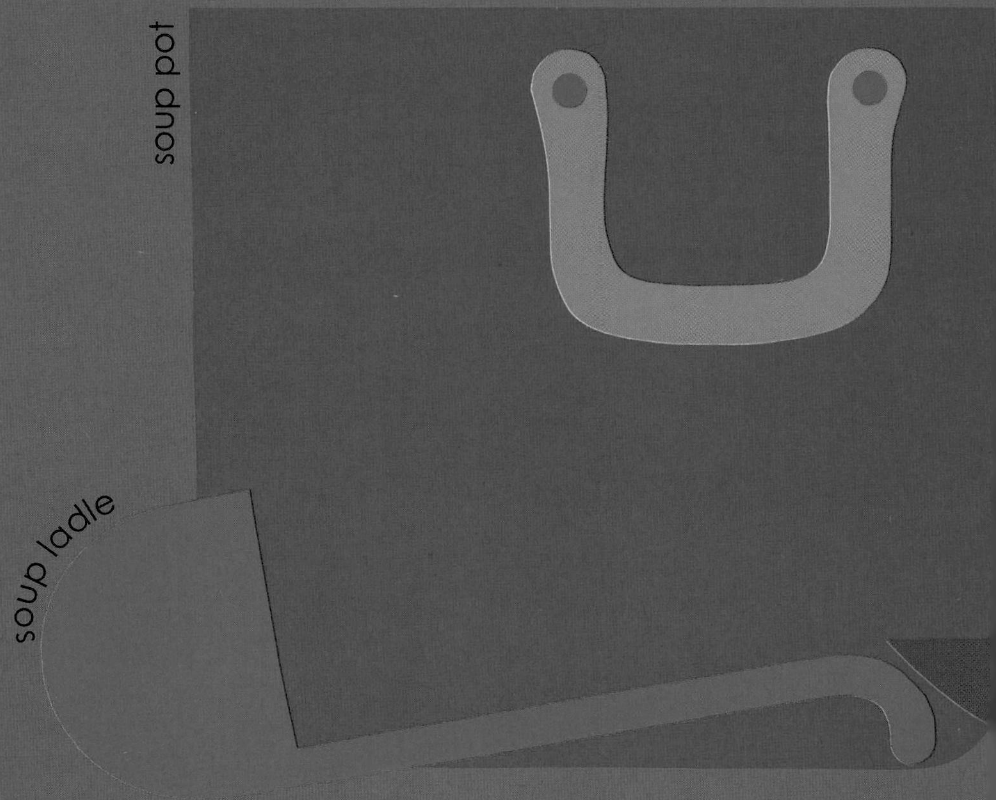

carrot
corn
zucchini squash
onion
tomato
pea
broccoli
potato
pepper
green bean
knife
cabbage

and cook them into vegetable soup!

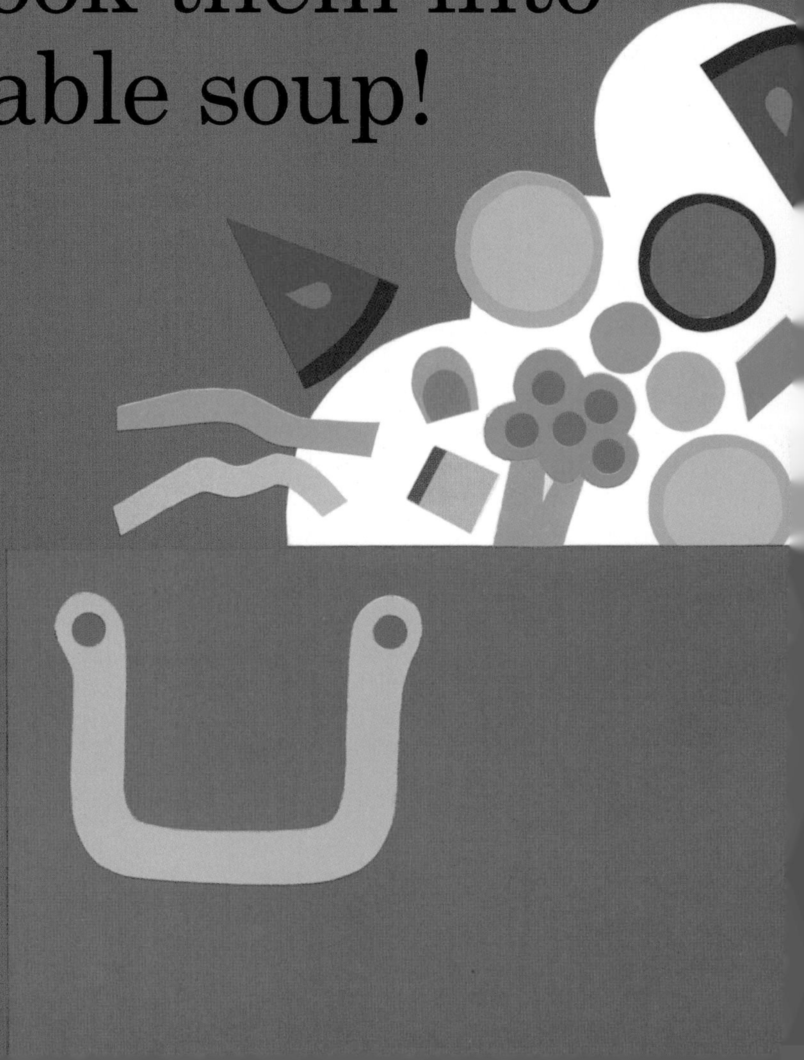

steam

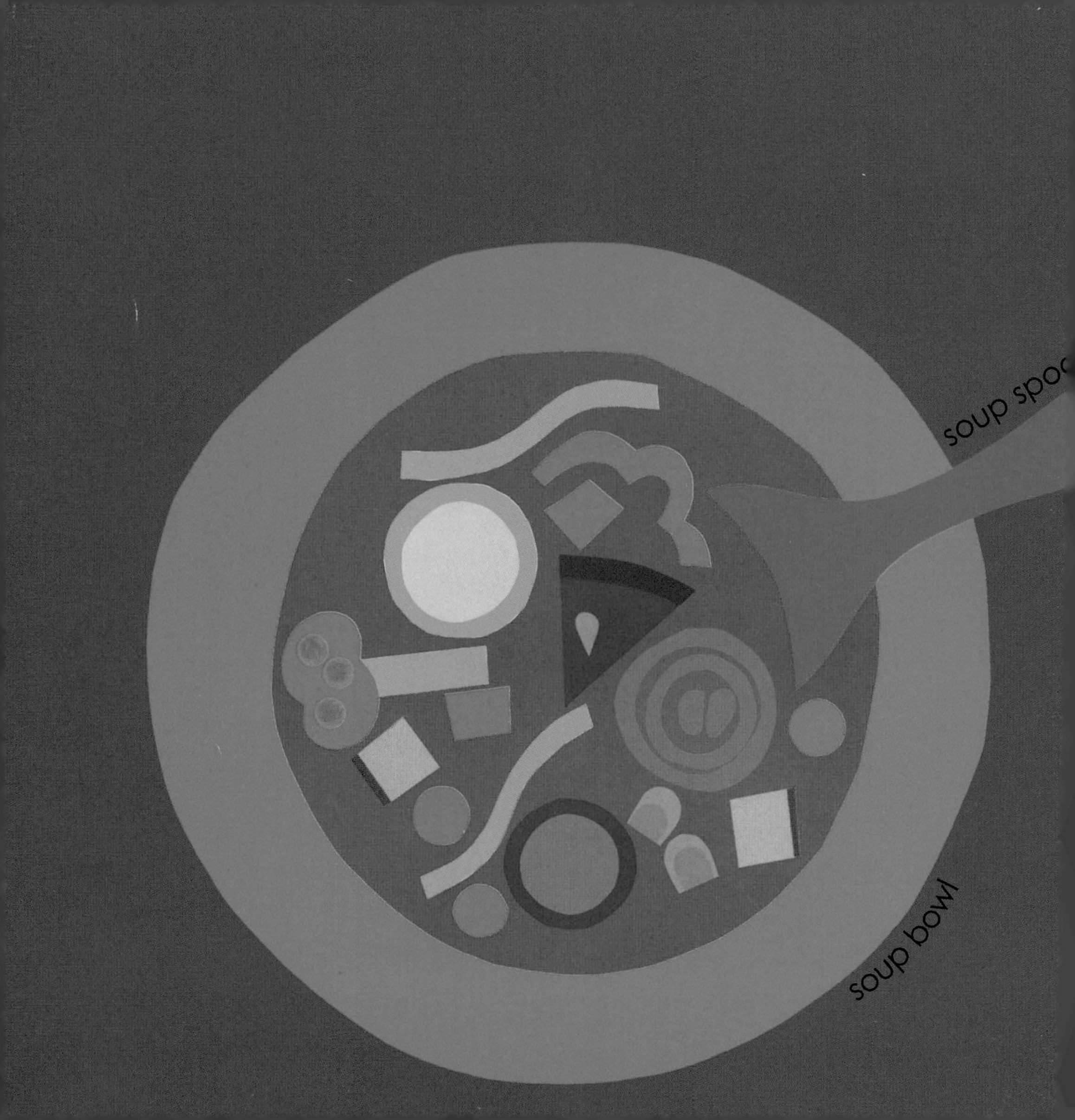
soup spoo
soup bowl

At last it's time
to eat it all up!

It was the best
soup ever . . .

and we can
grow it again
next year.

How to Make Vegetable Soup

1 Wash & cut:

1 large onion, peeled
2 carrots
1 medium potato, with skin
9 green beans, ends off
1/6 small head cabbage
1 stalk broccoli
3 medium tomatoes
1 small green pepper
1 zucchini (5 to 6 inches)
1 ear corn, husked

Slice onion and carrots into rounds. Cut potato into cubes and beans into 1-inch pieces. Chop cabbage wedge into shreds. Put in a large cooking pot. Set aside.

Slice broccoli stem into rounds; leave tops whole. Chop tomatoes into eighths. Cut out stem of green pepper and take out seeds; slice pepper into rounds, then into pieces. Slice zucchini into rounds. Cut corn off cob. Put in a bowl. Set aside.

2 Get ready:

4 bouillon cubes
5 cups water
1 big handful peas
1 bay leaf
½ cup snipped parsley
1 teaspoon dried marjoram
1 teaspoon dried thyme
salt & pepper to taste

3 Cook:

Add bouillon cubes and water to cooking pot with vegetables. Bring to boil. Reduce heat to medium-low and simmer, uncovered, 10 minutes.

Add peas. Add vegetables in bowl. Add herbs. Stir. Bring to simmer. Taste, then add salt and pepper. Stir. Simmer, uncovered, about 10 minutes longer, until vegetables are crisp-tender.

Makes 8 big servings or 12 small ones.

Food consultant: Peggy Daum